And the Cow Said Moo!

BY **MILDRED PHILLIPS**
PICTURES BY **SONJA LAMUT**

 Greenwillow Books

An Imprint of HarperCollinsPublishers

Egg tempera and oil paints were used for the full-color art.
The text type is Kabel Demi BT.
And the Cow Said Moo!
Text copyright © 2000 by Mildred Phillips
Illustrations copyright © 2000 by Sonja Lamut
Printed in Singapore by Tien Wah Press. All rights reserved.
http://harperchildrens.com

Library of Congress Cataloging-in-Publication Data

Phillips, Mildred.
And the cow said moo! /
by Mildred Phillips ;
pictures by Sonja Lamut.
p.   cm.
"Greenwillow Books."
Summary: A cow questions why the other animals
make their own sounds, instead of saying, "MOO!" as she does.
ISBN 0-688-16802-7 (trade).   ISBN 0-688-16803-5 (lib. bdg.)
[1. Animal sounds—Fiction.   2. Cows—Fiction.
3. Domestic animals—Fiction.   4. Identity—Fiction.]
I. Lamut, Sonja, ill.   II. Title.
PZ7.P546An   2000   [E]—dc21   99-14356   CIP

1 2 3 4 5 6 7 8 9 10 First Edition

For Meaghan, Ally,
& Madison B.
—M. P.

For my daughter, Anna
—S. L.

"Good morning, Sheep.
Say MOO! Say MOO!
If I say MOO, why don't you?"

"We **Ba-a-a**," said the sheep.
"That's what sheep do.
Ba-a-a!" said the sheep.
And the cow said, "**Moo!**"

Along came Duck.

"Good morning, Duck.
Say **Moo!** Say **Moo!**
If I say **Moo**, why don't you?"

"We **Quack!**" said the duck.
"That's what ducks do.
Quack-Quack!" said the duck.
"**Ba-a-a**," said the sheep.
And the cow said, "**Moo!**"

Along came Dog.

Oink Oink Oink Oink Oink Oink Oink Oink Oink Oink Oink Oink Oink Oink

Oink Oink Oink Oink Oink Oink Oink Oink Oink Oink Oink Oink Oink Oink

"Good morning, Pig.
Say **Moo!** Say **Moo!**
If I say **Moo**, why don't you?"

"We Oink!" said the pig.
"That's what pigs do.
Oink-Oink!" said the pig.
"Woof-Woof!" said the dog.
"Quack-Quack!" said the duck.
"Ba-a-a!" said the sheep.
And the cow said, "Moo!"

Along came Horse.

"Good morning, Horse.
Say **Moo!** Say **Moo!**
If I say **Moo**, why don't you?"

"We **Neigh!**" said the horse.
"That's what horses do.
Neigh!" said the horse.
"**Oink-Oink!**" said the pig.
"**Woof-Woof!**" said the dog.
"**Quack-Quack!**" said the duck.
"**Ba-a-a!**" said the sheep.
And the cow said, "**Moo!**"

Along came Owl.

"Good morning, Owl.
Say **Moo!** Say **Moo!**
If I say **Moo**, why don't you?"

"We **Whoooo**," said the owl.
"That's what owls do."

"Now if I said **Moo**,
and you said **Whoooo**,
you'd be me
and I'd be you!"

"I'm me!" said the cow.
"I'm a cow. I **Moo**.
I'm glad I am me
and I'm glad you are you."

"**Neigh!**" said the horse.
"*Oink-Oink!*" said the pig.
"**Woof-Woof!**" said the dog.
"**Quack-Quack!**" said the duck.
"*Ba-a-a!*" said the sheep.
The owl said, "**Whoooo**," . . .

and the cow said, "**Moo!**"